My Sound Parade

The Child's World

Published in the United States of America by The Child's World®
1980 Lookout Drive • Mankato, MN 56003-1705
800-599-READ • www.childsworld.com

ACKNOWLEDGMENTS
The Child's World®: Mary Berendes, Publishing Director
The Design Lab: Kathleen Petelinsek, Design and Page Production
Literacy Consultants: Cecilia Minden, PhD, and Joanne Meier, PhD

**LIBRARY OF CONGRESS
CATALOGING-IN-PUBLICATION DATA**
Moncure, Jane Belk.
  My sound parade / by Jane Belk Moncure;
illustrated by Rebecca Thornburgh.
    p. cm. — (Sound box books)
  Summary: "All the Sound Box characters join together for a
parade that features the letters of the alphabet."—Provided by
publisher.
  ISBN 978-1-60253-166-6 (library bound : alk. paper)
  [1. Stories in rhyme. 2. Alphabet. 3. Animals—Fiction. 4. Parades—
Fiction.] I. Thornburgh, Rebecca McKillip, ill. II. Title. III. Series.
  PZ8.3.M72My 2009
  [E]—dc22   2008033153

A NOTE TO PARENTS AND EDUCATORS:

Magic moon machines and five fat frogs are just a few of the fun things you can share with children by reading books with them. Reading aloud helps children in so many ways! It introduces them to new words, motivates them to develop their own reading skills, and expands their attention span and listening abilities. So it's important to find time each day to share a book or two . . . or three!

As you read with young children, you can help develop their understanding of how print works by talking about the parts of the book—the cover, the title, the illustrations, and the words that tell the story. As you read, use your finger to point to each word, modeling a gentle sweep from left to right.

Simple word games help develop important prereading skills, including an understanding of rhyme and alliteration (when words share the same beginning sound, such as "six" and "sand"). Try playing with words from a book you've just shared: "What other words start with the same sound as moon?" "Cat and hat, do those words rhyme?" The possibilities are endless—and so are the rewards!

My Sound Parade

WRITTEN BY JANE BELK MONCURE

ILLUSTRATED BY REBECCA THORNBURGH

Clap your hands. Tap your feet.

A parade is coming down the street!

Little  and an alligator

lead the way.

"You can come along, too,"

they say.

Here comes Little  with a baby baboon, and a bear on a bicycle with a balloon.

Little  rides a camel with a cat and a clown.

Little 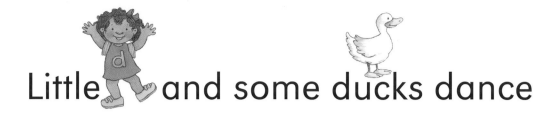 and some ducks dance

up and down.

Little  rides an elephant.

Some elves are in a box.

Here comes Little 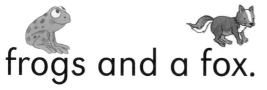 with five frogs and a fox.

Little  plays a guitar and sings a song. Some goats and a gorilla dance along.

Little 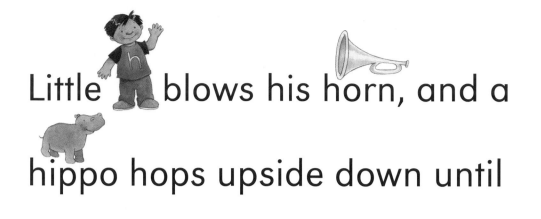 blows his horn, and a

hippo hops upside down until

he stops.

Little  skips along with her  insect zoo.

Little 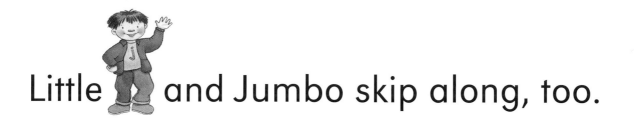 and Jumbo skip along, too.

Here comes Little  and
a kangaroo.

Little  will take you for a ride

with a lamb and a lion. Step inside!

Little  comes by with a moose and some mice. And three little monkeys. They are very nice.

Little  has nickels for everyone.

Little  and an ostrich join in

the fun.

Little  rides her pony with piglets three.

Little 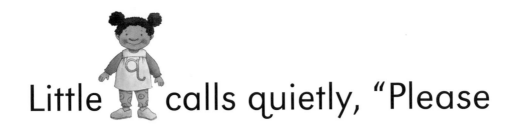 calls quietly, "Please

wait for me."

Little  has a reindeer. You can ride

it, too. . . with a rabbit and a rooster

singing "Cock-a-doodle-doo!"

Little  and a sailor skip along

with six silly seals singing a song.

Little  drives a truck with a

box full of toys.

Little  has umbrellas for all

the girls and boys.

Little  has lots of valentines

that say, "We like you."

Little  and her whale say, "We like you, too!"

Where are they going? Do not ask me.

Ask Little  X and y . . .

and 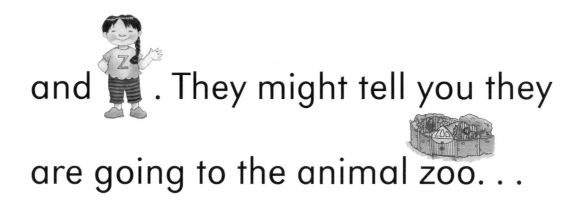. They might tell you they

are going to the animal zoo. . .

. . . the brand new Sound Box animal zoo!

pony

seals

whale

zebra

kangaroo

quail

moose

reindeer

nightingales

cat

yak

piglet

tiger

rhino

More to Do!

The sound parade was lots of fun! All our friends from the Sound Box books were there. After all that marching, everyone is hungry. You can make some Sound Parade Alphabet Soup to share with the Sound Box friends!

What you need:

- index cards or squares of construction paper
- pencils
- markers
- crayons
- scissors
- glue
- old magazines and catalogs
- a big bowl

Directions:

To make this silly soup, find pictures of foods that start with each letter. Look in old magazines or catalogs. Cut out the pictures and put them in your bowl. If you cannot find a picture of something, draw it on an index card or some construction paper. Imagine sharing the soup with your Sound Box friends!

Ideas for ingredients:

A: apples, artichokes, and avocados

B: bananas, barley, and beets

C: carrots, celery, and chocolate

D: donuts and drumsticks

Now you fill in the rest!